Yori and Yetta

BRAUNA B. HARRANT

Illustrated by Richard Max Kolding

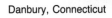

Grolier Enterprises Inc.,   Danbury, Connecticut

One day, some of the AlphaPets were eating lunch in Yori the Yucky Yak's yard. They were having peanut butter-and-jelly sandwiches, bananas, and apple juice. Of course, Yori was enjoying his favorite lunch of yam yogurt, pickled prunes, and an egg-white shake.

"Do you really like that yucky stuff?" Nelly the Naughty Newt asked.

"Sure do!" said Yori. "It may be yucky to you, but it's yummy to me. Yams make the yogurt taste sweet, and egg whites get nice and fluffy when you beat them—just like whipped cream. I save the yellow yolks for Yetta, my special pet spider. Yetta loves egg yolks."

As Tina the Truthful Tiger was about to take a bite of her sandwich, a bee came buzzing by.

"*Eek!*" cried Tina. "Get that bee away from me!"

Bradley the Brave Bear rolled up a newspaper and started to swat the bee.

"Hey! Don't do that!" yelled Yori. "That bee won't hurt you if you don't bother it."

"Yuck!" said Albert the Absent-minded Alligator. "I hate bees. They're awful!" So he grabbed his yo-yo and ran away from the table.

"Yes, awful!" repeated Monty the Mimicking Mouse as he followed Albert.

"I bet you like honey," Yori said to Bradley. "Bees make honey."

"Oh, I didn't think about that," Bradley said. "I really *do* love honey."

"That bee is collecting nectar from flowers to make honey," Yori said. "Nature is wonderful! There's a place and a purpose for just about everything."

"Never mind the bees," said Albert, rolling up his jeans. "Let's go wading."

"Good idea," said Tina.

"Mmm," said Queenie the Quiet Quail.

The AlphaPets followed Albert to Yori's pond and stepped into the water. But the water was muddy.

"Yuck," said Tina. "This feels slimy."

"Yuck," said Monty. "Slimy."

"Oh, but this mud feels so good squishing under my feet," Yori said. "Besides, lots of worms and snails live down here. I like to pick them up and let them wriggle on my arm. They tickle, you know."

"I wish you wouldn't say those awful things, Yori!" yelled Nelly. "Why do you like all this creepy, crawly, weird stuff? Why can't you be more like us?"

"Yes," agreed Monty. "Why can't you be more like us?"

Yori felt sad. He shook his head and said, "You just don't understand! Everything in nature has a place and a purpose."

Yori started walking back to his house. "I'm going inside," he whispered. "It's time to feed Yetta."

The AlphaPets watched as Yori closed the door.

"Yori treats Yetta as if she were a real pet," Bradley said. "He feeds her and plays with her and even takes her for walks."

"Imagine having a spider for a pet!" Albert said.

"Yori sure is yucky!" said Nelly.

"Sure is!" Monty said.

"Mmm," Queenie added.

The AlphaPets had started to play ball when Yori came running back into the yard. He looked very upset.

"I can't find Yetta!" he cried. "She's gone! I think she's lost! Yetta has never wandered off before! Please, help me find her."

The AlphaPets stopped playing and helped Yori.

They looked all around the house, near the pond, and in the yam patch. "Yetta! Yetta!" they called.

When they looked behind the barn, Tina spotted a big wasps' nest hanging from a beam.

"Wow!" yelled Tina. "Look at that wasps' nest!"

"Wasps are important," said Yori. "They help clean up dead trees and branches. As I said, everything in nature has its place and purpose."

As Yori turned around, he saw a big spider web on a nearby bush.

"I found her! *I found her!*" Yori shouted, and he ran over to the web. But the web was empty. Yori's heart sank. "This is the same kind of web Yetta weaves," he said. "I was sure Yetta would be here!"

"Yuck!" said Nelly. "Spider webs are *really* yucky."

"*Really* yucky!" said Monty.

"Not at all," Yori said. "Look closely, and you'll see how beautiful webs are. They look very fragile, but the threads are very strong."

"How do spiders learn to weave?" Tina asked.

"Spiders know how from the moment they're born," Yori explained. "Nobody has to teach them. And each type of spider makes a different kind of web. Of course, my Yetta makes the best."

"Hmm, that web *is* pretty. Look how it glistens in the sun," Queenie said.

As they came around the side of the barn, Albert jumped back. "What's that?" he asked, pointing to a strange-looking, squiggly shape near a rock.

"That's a snake's skin!" Yori said. He held it up to the sun. "See how pretty it is? When snakes grow they shed their skin. Their new skin is bigger and fits them better. It's like magic."

"But aren't snakes dangerous?" Nelly asked.

"Most snakes aren't dangerous," said Yori. "Some are poisonous, but many can be a real help to nature."

"The next thing you'll tell me is that worms are important, too!" Bradley said with a chuckle.

"They are!" Yori said. "They let air get into the soil and make it easier for flowers, fruits, and vegetables to grow. Remember, everything has its place and purpose. All little creatures are amazing if you take the time to understand them."

Yori and his friends sat down to rest.

"I wish I knew where my little Yetta was," Yori sighed.

"If you had a puppy for a pet instead of a yucky spider, you wouldn't have this problem," Nelly said.

"I guess I *do* like some things that you don't like," Yori said. "That may make me a little different, but it doesn't make me wrong!"

The AlphaPets got up and continued to look for Yori's beloved Yetta.

They looked under a big, flat rock and discovered a colony of busy ants. But they didn't find Yetta.

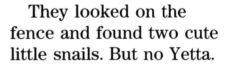

They looked on the fence and found two cute little snails. But no Yetta.

They looked near the water and saw a big box turtle. Still no Yetta.

They found cocoons and butterflies, grasshoppers, dragonflies, and lots of spotted ladybugs.

"Yetta! Yetta! Where are you?" they called. But Yetta was nowhere to be found.

Yori was about to give up his search when he noticed his friends at the side of the house, looking at something.

"What are you looking at?" he called to them.

"Come here, Yori!" Tina yelled. "Come here, quick!"

Yori ran over to take a look.

There, walking up the drainpipe, was Yetta!

And . . . following right behind her were five tiny spiders.

"Oh, how cute!" Bradley said.

"How adorable!" Queenie sighed.

"Now we know why Yetta wandered off!" Nelly said.
"To have her babies!"

"Hurray!" Yori cried. "This is amazing! Yetta is taking care of her babies! I always knew Yetta was a very special spider!"

Yori dashed into the house and brought out a big bowl of frozen yogurt.

"And now," Yori said, "we must celebrate Yetta's homecoming, her new babies, my good friends, and— most of all—Nature, which has a place and a purpose for all living things."

"Even you," Nelly said with a friendly laugh.

And all the AlphaPets laughed along with her.

There's a place and a purpose for all these words. Enjoy them with me.

yo-yo

yam

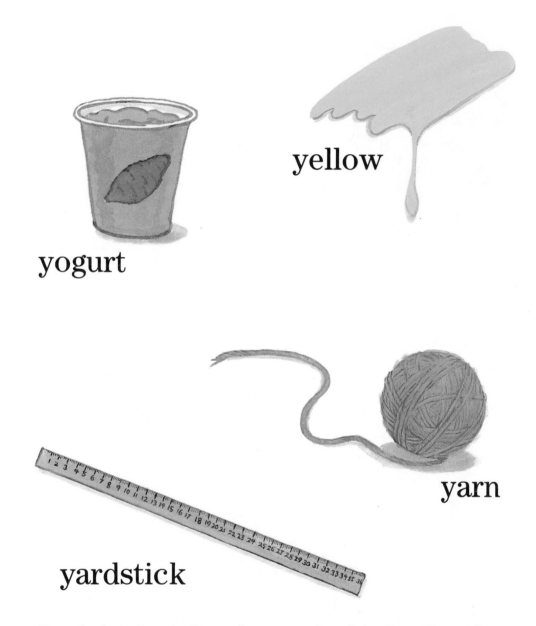

yellow

yogurt

yarn

yardstick

Look back at the pictures in this book and try to find these and other things that begin with the letter Y.

Know Your Alphabet

Aa Bb

Gg Hh

Mm Nn Oo Pp

Uu Vv Ww